Spy Hops
&
Belly Flops

Spy Hops
& Belly Flops

Curious Behaviors of Woodland Animals

Lynda Graham-Barber • *illustrated by* Brian Lies

Houghton Mifflin Company
Boston 2004

If you like to wiggle, hop, and stomp,
Come join us on an animal romp.
Crouch and jump, flap and fly,
Let's go see what the animals spy.

Quick—jump up like
the curious spy hopper.

A red fox hops up on its back legs to watch the animals along the river.

Slide on your tummy like
a sleek belly flopper.

Whoosh! The playful otters whiz down the muddy bank on their
smooth bellies.

Step into the water and look
for plants like the bog wader.

The long-legged bull moose wades into the water to scoop up tender plants.

Hold your food in your hands and
nibble like the clever raider.

Holding it with its sensitive fingers, the masked raccoon munches a corncob
it has raided from the farmer's field.

Ready, set, jump into a puddle like a noisy splasher.

The belted kingfisher leaves its perch, makes a loud rattling call, then dives headfirst into the water to spear a fish.

Flap your hands behind you
like a nervous tail flasher.

When alarmed, the leaping white-tailed deer raises its tail and springs off,
while the baby fawn follows its parent's white "flag."

**Thump your foot lightly—
you're a patient toe tapper.**

The wood turtle thumps its foot on the soft, damp earth, then eats the earthworms that wiggle to the surface.

**Knock on wood like a
hungry bill rapper.**

High in a beech tree, a pileated woodpecker drills its strong, sharp bill deep
into the bark to find insects.

Buzz near a flower like the brilliant darting hummer.

Up, down, forward, backward—like a helicopter—the ruby-throated hummingbird sips flower nectar, rapidly beating its tiny wings.

Stand tall and flap your arms—
you're a distant drummer.

On a hollow log, the ruffed grouse spreads its tail and pumps its wings,
making a sound like a lawn mower starting up.

Can you puff up your cheeks
like the busy cheek packer?

A chipmunk's cheeks puff up like balloons as it stuffs nine nuts in its mouth, four in each pouch and one between its front teeth.

Can you grind and chew slowly
like the prickly tree snacker?

Along the stream, a porcupine strips off cedar bark to eat the sweet sapwood.

Blink your eyes—open-close-open—
you're a flashing strober.

On a warm evening, male and female fireflies flash their lights, filling the
meadow with a twinkling glow.

Poke around on the ground
like the hungry mud prober.

In the same meadow, a woodcock pokes its needlelike bill into the damp
ground to find earthworms.

Open your arms and twist-turn
like the swooping beepers.

Dip-diving over the night marsh, furry bats make high-pitched beeps that
locate insects and help the bats catch dinner.

Listen! Do you hear the jingle
of the tiny spring peepers?

Below in the cattails, the sound of faint bells jingle as thousands of inch-long male peepers whistle to attract mates.

Raise your head and call out
like the pack howler.

Up on the mountain, the timber wolf howls to find its family.

Crouch low and wait
like a stalking prowler.

Waiting silently, crouching, quietly stalking, the bobcat pounces on a hare.

Ready? Take one long jump like the big-footed hopper.

The snowshoe hare races across the field, leaping twelve feet in one hop, bounding on its large, snowshoe-shaped back feet.

**Run for cover like the
hard-working timber dropper.**

Down in the swamp, a beaver cuts away wood with its two chisel-like teeth,
then scrambles off before the poplar crashes to the ground.

**Stretch your arms wide
to parachute glide.**

Like a handkerchief caught in the wind, the flying squirrel glides from tree branch to branch through the evening sky.

Climb up and hold tight
for a piggyback ride.

Below, a baby opossum leaves its mother's warm pouch and crawls onto her
back with its brothers and sisters for a bedtime ride.

Cry out loudly and swoop:
you're a flapping deep-woods hooter.

Hoo, hoo-oo. Flying high over a pine grove, the great horned owl plunges
down to carry off a skunk in its powerful talons and beak.

Click your teeth and stomp, just like the hissing shooter.

When a skunk is threatened, it chatters its teeth, stomps the ground, then twists its back around and shoots out a smelly spray.

You've now flopped and hopped as the animals do.
Are you tired? Did you learn something new?
Thump, thump, whoosh, splash—wheeeeeee!
Which of the animals would you most like to be?

For Ray, ever vigilant, and for David, ever playful
—L.G.-B.

For Anna Keith Anderson, James Anderson,
and Merle Vivian Keith —B.L.

Text copyright © 2004 by Lynda Graham-Barber
Illustrations copyright © 2004 by Brian Lies

www.houghtonmifflinbooks.com

The text of this book is set in Berkeley.

Library of Congress Cataloging-in-Publication Data
Graham-Barber, Lynda.
Spy hops and belly flops : curious behaviors of woodland animals /
by Lynda Graham-Barber ; illustrated by Brian Lies.
p. cm.
Summary: Invites the reader to observe forest animals and copy such behaviors as jumping into a puddle
like a diving kingfisher, tapping a foot like a wood turtle, and buzzing near a flower like a hummingbird.
ISBN 0-618-22291-X
1. Forest animals—Behavior—Juvenile literature. [1. Forest animals. 2. Animals—Habits and behavior.]
I. Lies, Brian, ill. II. Title.
QL112.G7 2004   591.73—dc21   2003005392

Printed in Singapore
TWP 10 9 8 7 6 5 4 3 2 1